SHORT TA...
Fables

The Tortoise
and the
Hare

Adapted by Shannon Eric Denton

Illustrated by Mark Pennington

WAYLAND

WAYLAND

First published in 2013 by Wayland

Copyright © 2013 Wayland

Wayland
338 Euston Road
London NW1 3BH

Wayland Australia
Level 17/207 Kent Street
Sydney, NSW 2000

Adapted Text by Shannon Eric Denton
Illustrations by Mark Pennington
Colours by Robby Bevard
Edited by Stephanie Hedlund
Interior Layout by Kristen Fitzner Denton and Alyssa Peacock
Book Design and Packaging by Shannon Eric Denton
Cover Design by Alyssa Peacock

Copyright © 2008 by Abdo Consulting Group

A cataloguing record for this title is available at the British Library.
Dewey number: 398.2'452-dc23

Printed in China

ISBN: 978 0 7502 7784 6

Wayland is a division of Hachette Children's Books, an Hachette UK company.
www.hachette.co.uk

One sunny day, a hare sat by a tree.

The hare watched a tortoise approach.

The tortoise was slow.

The hare laughed at the slow tortoise.

'You're the slowest thing I've ever seen!' the hare said.

'You shouldn't make fun of me' said the tortoise.

13

'There is nothing you can do about it' the hare said.

'Do you want to race?' asked the tortoise.
The hare couldn't stop laughing.

The hare agreed, and soon they were racing.

The hare ran very far ahead of the tortoise.

22

'You'll never catch me' laughed the hare.

The hare grew tired and decided to take a nap.

27

While the hare slept, the tortoise slowly continued.

FINI

When the hare woke up, the tortoise was crossing the finish line!

The moral of the story is:

Slow and steady wins the race!

SHORT TALES
Fairy Tales

Titles in the Short Tales Fairy Tales series:

Aladdin and the Lamp

978 0 7502 7750 1

Beauty and the Beast

978 0 7502 7752 5

Jack and the Beanstalk

978 0 7502 7751 8

Puss in Boots

978 0 7502 7754 9

Sleeping Beauty

978 0 7502 7755 6

The Little Mermaid

978 0 7502 7753 2

WAYLAND
www.waylandbooks.co.uk

Follow us on Twitter @waylandbooks | Find us on Facebook Wayland Books

SHORT TALES
Fables

Titles in the Short Tales Fables series:

The Ants and the Grasshopper

978 0 7502 7756 3

The Boy Who Cried Wolf

978 0 7502 7757 0

The Fox and the Grapes

978 0 7502 7758 7

The Lion and the Mouse

978 0 7502 7783 9

The Tortoise and the Hare

978 0 7502 7784 6

The Town Mouse and the Country Mouse

978 0 7502 7785 3

WAYLAND
www.waylandbooks.co.uk

Follow us on Twitter @waylandbooks | Find us on Facebook Wayland Books